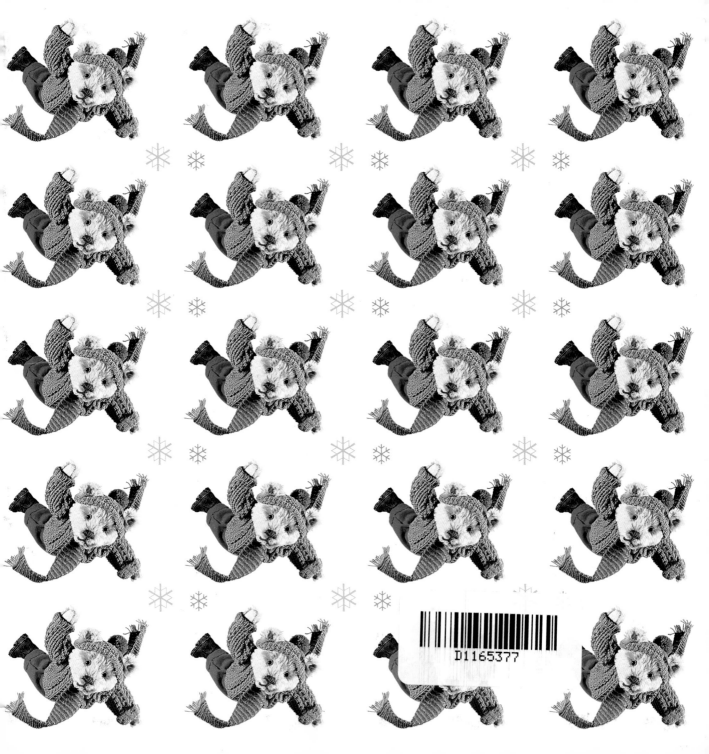

A DK Publishing Book

Senior Designer   Claire Jones
Senior Editor   Caryn Jenner
Editor   Fiona Munro
US Editor   Kristin Ward
Production   Katy Holmes
Photography   Dave King

First American Edition, 1997
2 4 6 8 10 9 7 5 3 1

Published in the United States by
DK Publishing, Inc.
95 Madison Avenue
New York, New York 10016

Visit us on the World Wide Web at: http://www.dk.com

A catalog record is available from the Library of Congress.

ISBN 0-7894-1414-7

Reproduced in Italy by G.R.B. Graphica, Verona
Printed and bound in Italy by L.E.G.O.

Acknowledgments
DK would like the thank the following manufacturers
for permission to photograph copyright material:
Ty, Inc. for "Toffee" the dog

DK would also like to thank
Patricia Tregunno, Vera Jones, Robert Fraser and Dave King
for their help with props and set design.

Can you find
the little bear
in each scene?

P.B. BEAR

The Snowy Ride

Lee Davis

One cold winter morning P.B. Bear looked
out the window. He cleared away the mist
with his paw, and then he saw...
...snow!
"Yippee!" he shouted. "It's snowing!"
Outside, the snow made the yard sparkle.
P.B. Bear started to get dressed.
He put on his warmest winter sweater,
his socks,
and his boots.
Then he put on
his woolly scarf and hat.

P.B. Bear went outside. The cold air made his face tingle.
Just as he was wondering what snowy game to play,
Dermott arrived. He was pulling a sled.
"Come on, P.B.!" said Dermott. "Let's go sledding!"
"Oh, yes!" said P.B. "Let's go down the hill!"
Together, the two friends walked through the snow,
with the sled *slipping* and *sliding* behind them.

They pulled the
sled to the top
of the hill.
"Are you ready?"
called Dermott.
"READY, SET, GO!"
replied P.B. Bear.

Dermott gave the sled a mighty push
and hopped onto the back.
Down the hill they went,
until —
almost before
they knew it —

they were at the bottom!

There was another hill nearby that was much bigger.
"Look! There's Dorothy," said P.B.
Dermott's big sister, Dorothy, was sledding
down the big hill. She went very fast.
"We're too little for the big hill," said Dermott.
"*I'm* not too little," said P.B. Bear, and he pulled
the sled right up to the top of the big hill.

Down the big hill went P.B. —
faster and faster!
He wanted to stop, but the sled kept going —
faster and faster!
Suddenly, the sled went over a BUMP...

and P.B. Bear went flying through the air!

P.B. landed in a big snowdrift.
BRRRRRRR! He shivered.
The snow was cold.
The snow was wet.
But at least it was soft!
P.B. wriggled around
and tried to get up.
The snow was slippery, too!

Dermott and Dorothy ran as fast as
they could to the snowdrift.
"Are you all right, P.B.?" asked Dermott.
"That was a very fast ride!" said Dorothy.
"Yes, I know," said P.B. Bear. "A little too fast."
Dermott and Dorothy helped
P.B. out of the snowdrift.
He had snow in his ears,
    on his nose,
        inside his sweater,
            and inside his boots!
                "I've got snow everywhere!"
                he laughed.

Dorothy, Dermott, and P.B. set off through
the snow for home, with their sleds
slipping and *sliding* behind them.

One day P.B. Bear would be big enough
to sled down the big hill.
But for now, the little hill
was just the right size!

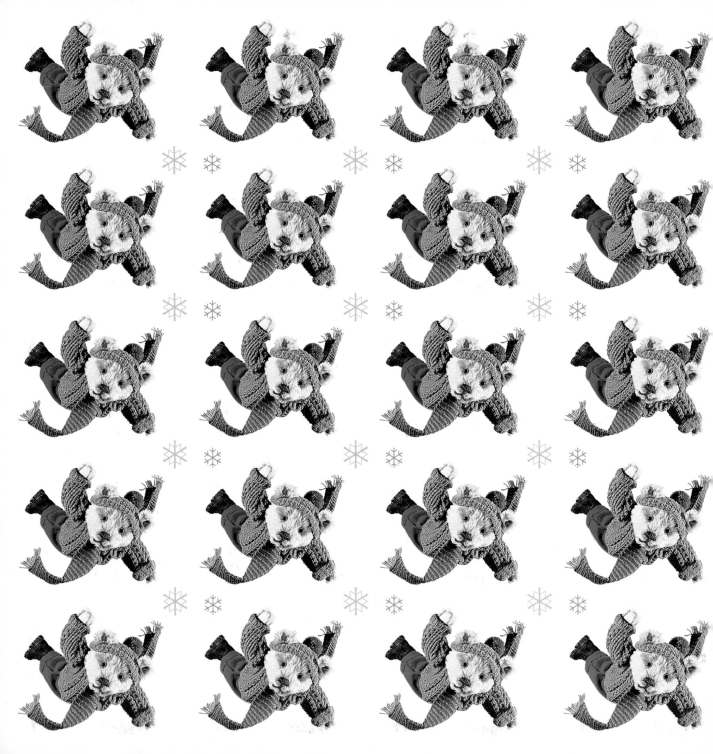